Nellie TO THE Rescue

STORY BY
Julie Starkey

ILLUSTRATED BY
Lisa Townsend

Story by Julie Starkey.

All illustrations by Lisa Townsend. All illustrations copyright of Lisa Townsend.

Cover design and interior layout by Krysta Maria Micallef of www.xorxcreative.com from original illustrations by Lisa Townsend.

To my Father and Greta

Brownie was doing it rough and her hunger
was constant.

She was the mother of four growing puppies who
rolled and tumbled in the red dirt beside her.

Each day she left her puppies beneath the shady snappy gums, hidden from view between big red rocks.

In the nearby town, Brownie roamed the streets and scavenged the rubbish dump for scraps of food. She found just enough to make milk for her puppies.

On her return they charged out to greet her,
with Nellie, the boldest puppy, in the lead.
They gleefully pulled at Brownie's ears and
nipped at her legs as they jostled for a teat.

One day Brownie returned to her waiting
puppies, unaware that she had been followed.

The shadow of a tall ranger fell over their
haven. Brownie shrank back into a corner and
the puppies hid behind her.

The ranger sat down nearby, speaking softly
and offering Brownie food.

Brownie ate quickly and sat back to regard the ranger.

She sensed his kindness, and allowed him to reach for brave Nellie, who was edging towards him. One by one the ranger lifted the whole family into his ute and drove them to the city pound.

Nothing at the pound was familiar.

The concrete floor was hard and cold.
Once a day, Brownie and her pups ate the
dry biscuits they were given, and once a day
a big hose flooded their cage.

Dogs they didn't know howled, growled,
whined and barked. Dogs came and dogs went.

The ranger soon saw that these
friendly pups and their mother
would make wonderful pets.

He rang the SAFE team.

Hundreds of kilometres away, in the south
of the land, a son came in from his garden
and tucked a rug in snugly around his
father's lap.

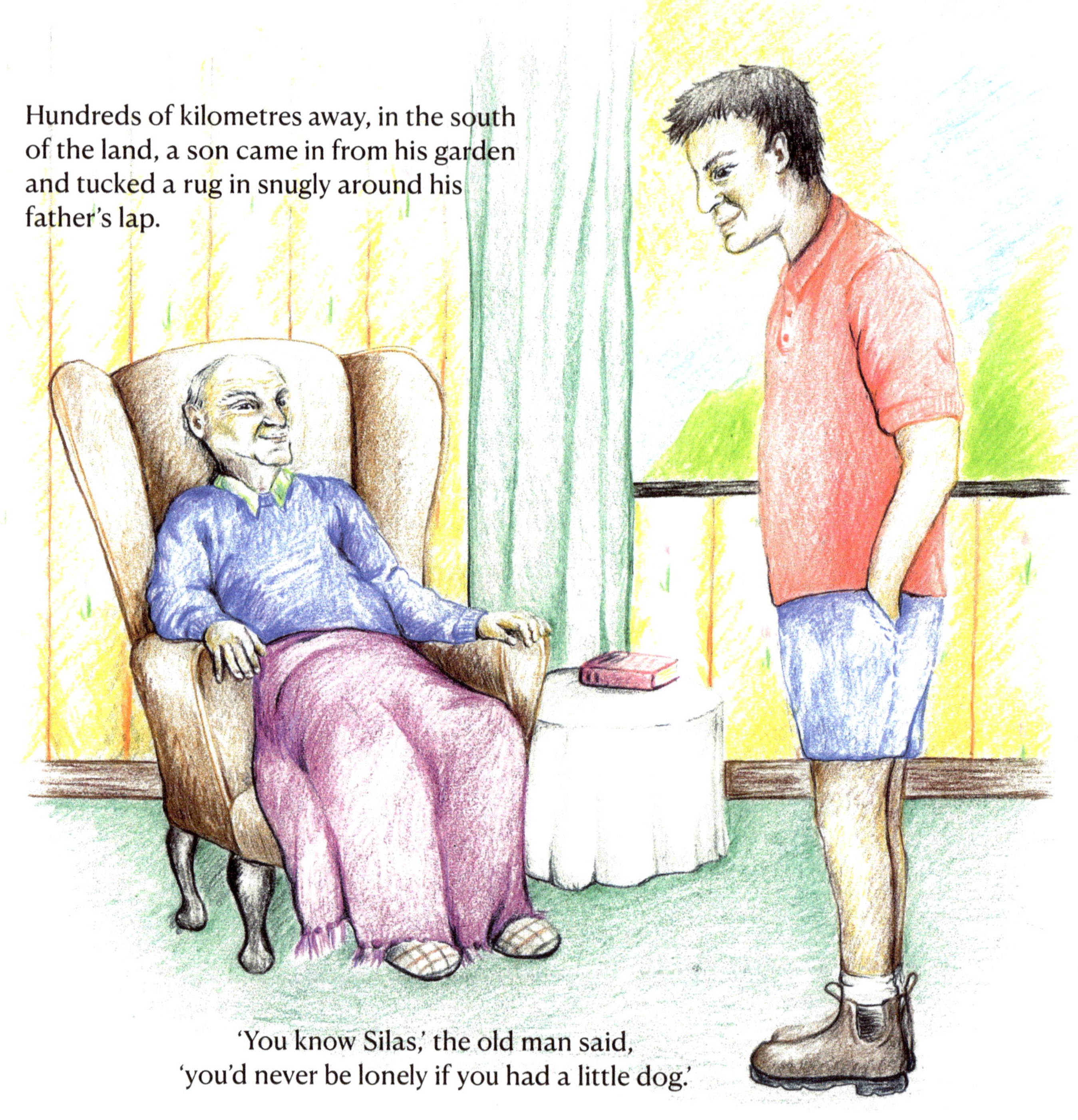

'You know Silas,' the old man said,
'you'd never be lonely if you had a little dog.'

Silas smiled and returned
to digging his garden bed, wondering,
'Is this Dad's way of saying that *he* wants a little dog?'

SAFE soon found different foster homes
for Brownie and her strong and independent
puppies. Brownie wagged them all goodbye.

Away from her mother, at first Nellie did not feel
so bold. But she was ever eager to please. She learnt
how to play Frisbee with the children, and even
made friends with the cat.

As the weeks went by, Brownie and her pups
moved on from their foster homes. One by one,
they were adopted by people seeking rescue dogs
to be their companions. All, that is, except Nellie.

She was waiting for the right home.

SIMBA
NELLIE
DIESEL
MILO
MISTY
INDY

Meanwhile, down the road, a bloke named Hank
decided that he wanted a dog.

He went to the SAFE website and trawled through
the photos of dogs waiting for a home – there
were handsome dogs and fancy dogs and hounds
of all sorts, but one alert puppy with big brown
eyes stood out.

The next day, SAFE rang Nellie's foster home
and arranged for Hank to visit.

As soon as he sat down on the garden chair,
Nellie ran up and licked his hand, sniffed his shoes
carefully, wagged her tail and promptly lay down
on his foot.

That was enough for Hank. He filled out SAFE's
adoption forms: Did his home have a good-sized
yard; did it have a fence; was there enough shade?
Tick, tick, tick.

'Come on Nellie, let's go. We'll make a life together.'

SAFE
We need you
Fostering Saves Lives
Relinquishment Form

But three months later, Hank, with downcast
eyes, re-entered the SAFE office with Nellie at
his side. Her tail was still.

'I've got a new girlfriend,' Hank explained,

'she has two large dogs and they are giving Nellie
a really hard time. It's just not working out.'

The SAFE team understood.

'Thanks for making Nellie's happiness a priority.
Don't worry, we'll find another good home for her.'

Hundreds of kilometres away, in the south
of the land, a son gave his father a serviette
as he removed the lunch tray from his lap.

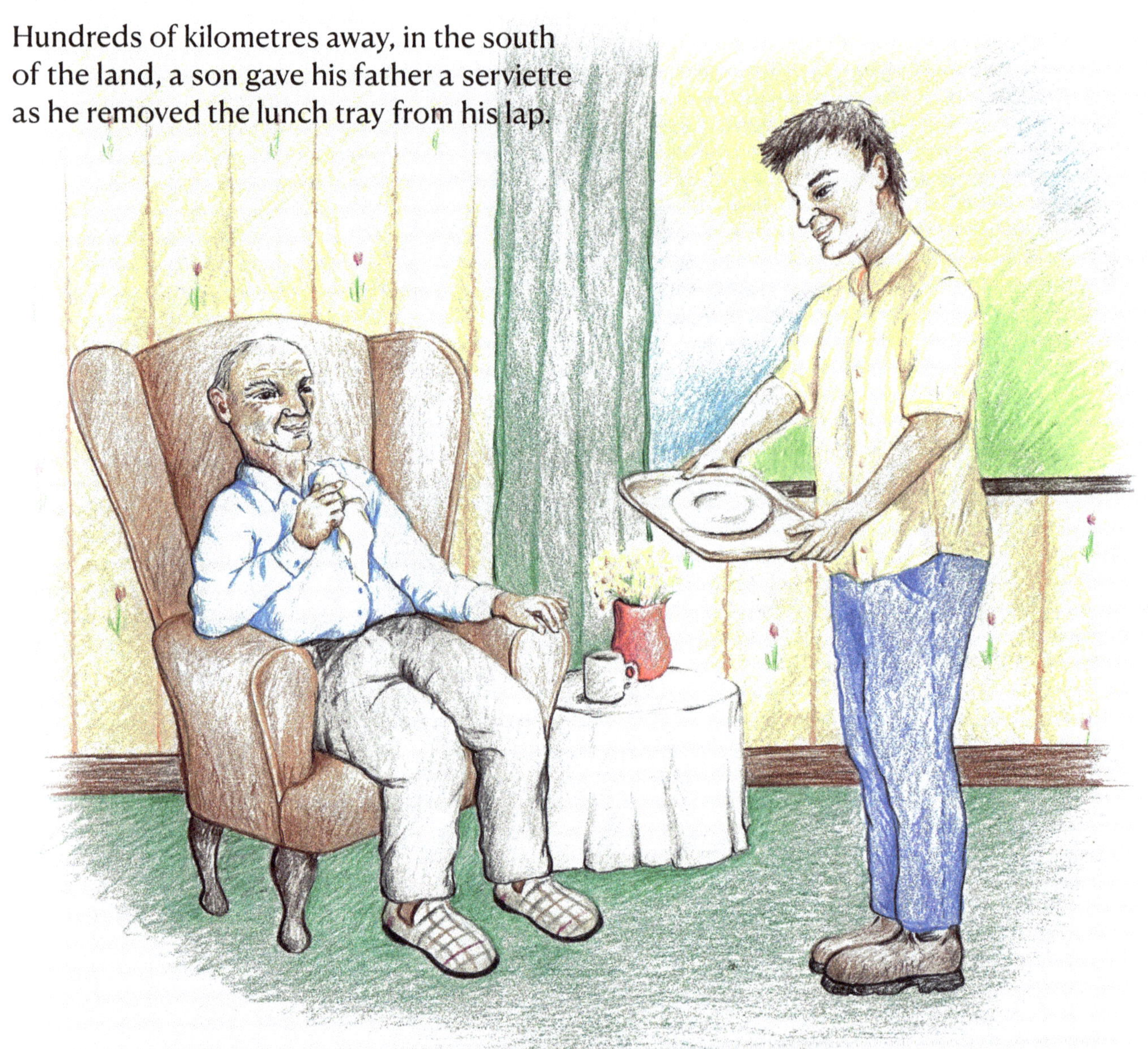

'You know Silas,' the old man said,
'you'd never be lonely if you had a little dog.'

Silas smiled and returned
to cleaning out the shed, wondering,
'Is this Dad's way of telling me that *he's* lonely?'

Back in SAFE foster care, Nellie made the best of things. She missed Hank, but she didn't miss those two bully-boy dogs.

One day, Grace and Charlie came to meet her. They patted her and she wagged her tail, but then they left. They wanted a bigger dog.

Another day, Sally and George came to meet her. They patted her and she wagged her tail, but then they left.

They wanted a fluffier dog.

Finally, a boy called Sam came with his
parents. Sam jumped up and down
with excitement and Nellie joined in
the fun, wagging her tail joyously.

They ran and rolled together.

Sam and his parents left, but then they came back!
They wanted this very dog.

From winter to spring, and summer to autumn,
Nellie was happy in her new family. She was Sam's
dog and they stuck close together.

But one grey day, Nellie's world turned upside down again.

Sam's parents separated. Sam and his mother went
to live with friends, and his father was off to work in
the mines. Nobody could take Nellie with them.

Once again, SAFE welcomed Nellie back.
Two years had passed, and she was no longer a puppy.

Sam's father knelt down to pat her one last time.
Her tail was still. He said to the SAFE team, 'I'm so
sorry. We love Nellie but we just can't keep her.'

The SAFE team understood.
'You've done the right thing,' they said.
'She's a top little dog and we'll do all we can to find her another happy home.'

Hundreds of kilometres away, in the south of the land, a young woman changed the radio station for her father-in-law.

'You know, Martha,' the old man said,
'you and Silas would never be lonely if you had a little dog.'

Martha smiled and went to find Silas.
'I think you are right,' she said quietly.
'Dad needs a little dog.'

So, hundreds of kilometres away, in the south
of the land, the little family sat down together
and looked at SAFE's website.

Of all the dogs, they chose Nellie.

She was small; she was calm; she was friendly
– she was just right for them. But she was a
long way away – she would have to fly!

They filled out the adoption forms, and soon
Nellie's flight was booked.

AIR FREIGHT

The airport was noisy and strange. Nellie curled her tail underneath her and crouched on her own rug in the transport crate. She looked through the wire door with huge eyes as a man carried her to the plane.

She couldn't help shivering.

Rufus, the dog in the crate beside her, was quiet and confident. He had travelled before and knew the ropes. The journey was long. After a while, Nellie stopped shivering and went to sleep.

When they got to their destination, Rufus was
bouncing in anticipation. His tail was wagging
and his saliva drooling as a family came
towards him, calling his name.

Nellie watched, her tail still.

Then a gentle voice
spoke beside her.

'Welcome Nellie.

You have come such a long
way. Well done. Well done.'

Nellie sniffed the man's
brown hand. Her tail
started to wag.

Not far away, in the south of the land, an old man
woke from his snooze outside in the sun, one large
hand resting gently on his little dog's soft, warm body.

'You know,' the old man said to Martha and Silas,
'You two would never be lonely if you had a little dog.'

Martha smiled at Silas and patted her tummy.
'Maybe in a year or two,' she said, 'we might just need another little dog.'

About SAFE

SAVING ANIMALS FROM EUTHANASIA INC.

SAFE (Saving Animals from Euthanasia Inc.) was founded in Karratha, Western Australia in 2003 to address the lack of animal rescue services and now has branches across the state. Since its inception thousands of homeless animals have been rescued and rehomed.

Based on a foster care model, cats and dogs find love and care in homes, so do not have to suffer the isolation and separation anxiety often caused by being confined.

Attitudes around housing animals in shelters are shifting. No matter how well a shelter is run, the environment is an institutionalised one and not the same as a home environment. My vision is that in years to come foster homes will provide care for the majority and time in a shelter will be minimal.

The story of Nellie has been designed to help children accept inevitable life changes, and to witness, through Nellie the rescue pup, how well she managed the changes that life presented to her. It also highlights the vital role that animals play in our lives and shows, in the end, how Nellie was not the only one rescued.

Sue Hedley OAM
FOUNDER SAFE INC

www.safe.org.au

Acknowledgements

I am very grateful to Julie Starkey for the generous donation of her story of Nellie's journey.

Julie has had a connection to SAFE since her family adopted their dog, Ruby in the early days of SAFE. Her first book, "SAFE Ruby" tells the story of Ruby the homeless dog who had a few homes that didn't work out before settling into her family's home. Nellie's story has a similar theme but has added more depth that captures SAFE's growth as a rescue service. Thanks must also go to Julie's editor, Juliet Middleton.

Our illustrator, Lisa Townsend has been a dedicated SAFE team member for years and her passion is reflected in her artwork. Lisa's years in rescue shine through in her illustrations where she brings the story to life by the depth of her understanding and compassion for those who can't speak for themselves.

Thank you to Ian Hooper of The Book Reality Experience for his supportive guidance throughout the publishing process and to my friend Trish O'Neill who has taken on the challenge of coordinating the project.

Finally, I want to acknowledge a remarkable SAFE Team for their dedicated time, passion and ongoing care for the homeless cats and dogs who rely on us to save their lives.

We all trust that "Nellie to the Rescue" will help to bring much needed support in the way of volunteers and donations to SAFE.

The proceeds of the sale of this book will go to continuing the work of SAFE.